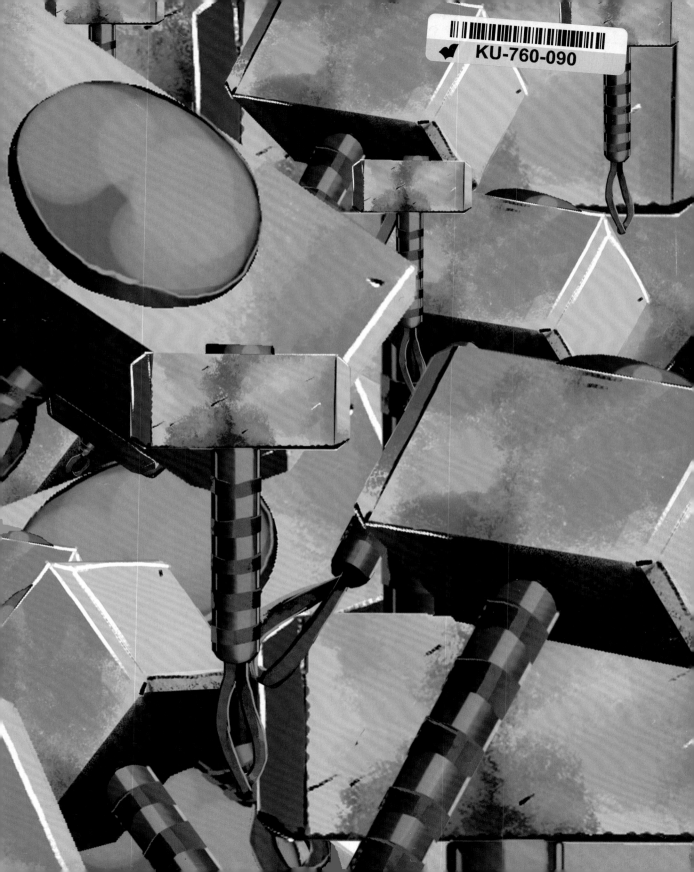

MARVEL
THOR™

AN ORIGIN STORY

Based on the Marvel comic book series **Thor**
Adapted by **Rich Thomas**
Illustrated by **The Storybook Art Group**
Cover illustrated by **Pat Olliffe** *and* **Brian Miller**

Bath • New York • Singapore • Hong Kong • Cologne • Delhi
Melbourne • Amsterdam • Johannesburg • Shenzhen

This edition published by Parragon in 2014
Parragon
Chartist House
15–17 Trim Street
Bath BA1 1HA, UK
www.parragon.com

ISBN 978-1-4723-2754-3

Printed in China

What would it be like to live among legends?
To be something more than human?

To hold great power in your hands ...

and know how to use it?

To be feared?

To be brave.

To be honoured.

To be
MIGHTY?

Some are born with these qualities.

And some spend their lives working to attain them.

This is a story about someone who was born into royalty, but needed to earn his honour.

This is a story about a hero ...

named THOR.

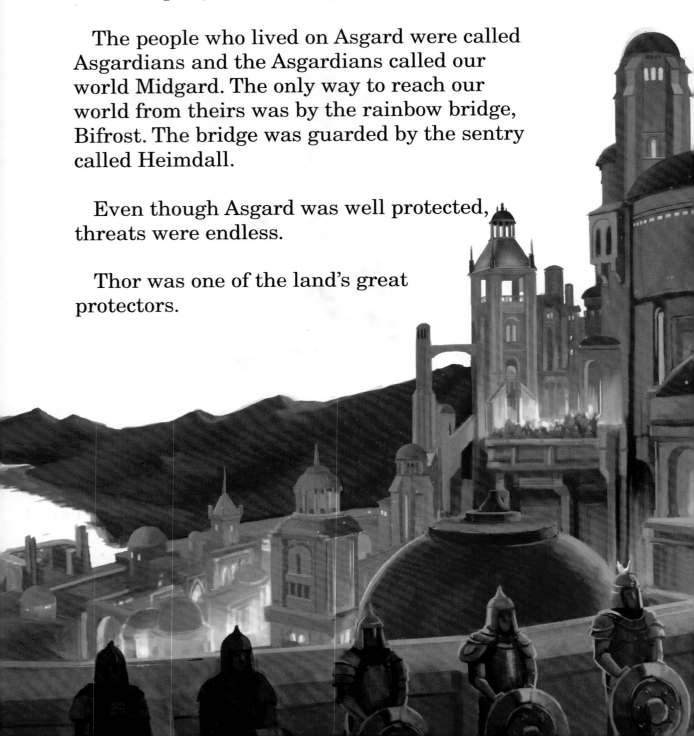

Thor's realm was called Asgard. It sat like an island where the shores were swept by the sea of space.

The people who lived on Asgard were called Asgardians and the Asgardians called our world Midgard. The only way to reach our world from theirs was by the rainbow bridge, Bifrost. The bridge was guarded by the sentry called Heimdall.

Even though Asgard was well protected, threats were endless.

Thor was one of the land's great protectors.

He was also a prince. He lived with his brother Loki in the castle of their father, Odin.

Thor was arrogant and chose his friends for their loyalty: the brave warrior Balder and a band of soldiers called the Warriors Three – Fandral, Volstagg and Hogun – and the beautiful, strong and wise Lady Sif.

Thor's father, Odin, ruled over all of Asgard.

He and his wife, Frigga, wanted nothing
more than for their sons to grow up to be worthy rulers.

But there could only be one supreme ruler of Asgard.
Only one who could be like Odin. And even though
Loki was thoughtful, clever and quick ...

Thor was firstborn and so the throne was his by right.

To determine when Thor would be ready to rule, Odin had a special hammer made. It was forged from a mystical metal called Uru, which came from the heart of a dying star.

The hammer was named Mjolnir and it held great power.

But no one would be able to lift the hammer unless he or she was worthy.

The hammer was immovable to Thor.

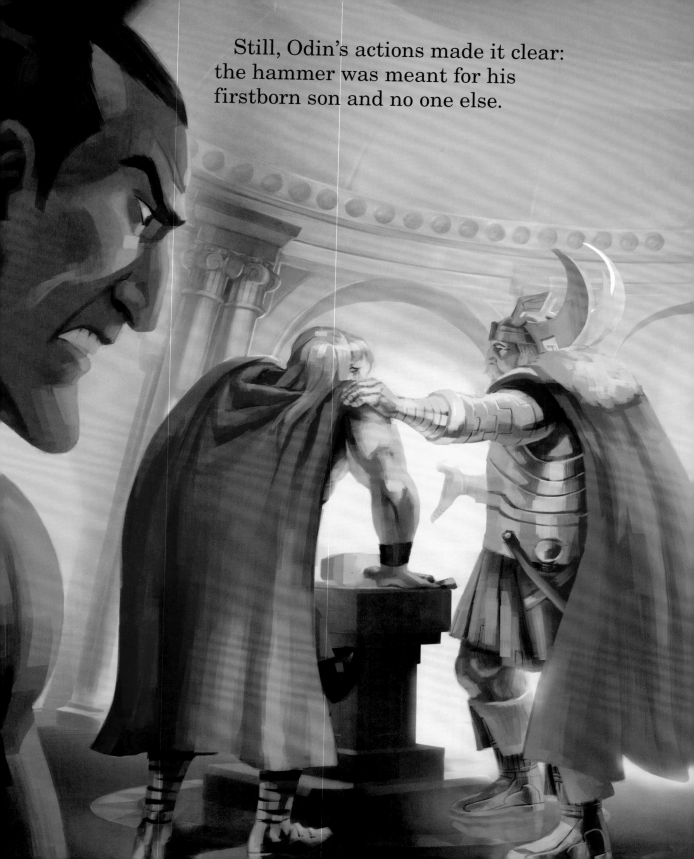

Still, Odin's actions made it clear:
the hammer was meant for his
firstborn son and no one else.

Even so, proving worthy of Mjolnir was not an easy task.

Thor spent nearly every moment trying to earn his right to hold the hammer. He performed amazing acts of bravery,

he was honoured for
acts of nobility ...

and he demonstrated
feats of great strength ...

and honour.

With every great achievement, Thor attempted once more to pick up Mjolnir. It seemed as if he would never raise the hammer more than a few inches from the table.

And then

one day ...

he DID.

Thor had proven himself worthy
of his weapon and he used it well.
When he threw the hammer, it
always returned to him.

When he twirled it by its handle,
he could soar like a winged beast!

And when he slammed it
twice upon the ground ...

he could summon all the power of
lightning, rain and thunder!

In fact, with his hammer in hand,
there was little Thor could not do.

And he knew it.

Odin wanted him to be a great warrior and he had become one. His father wanted him to earn the respect of Asgard. He had it. But then Thor began to let the power go to his head.

And Odin was not happy.

In fact, he had grown quite angry with his son.

Odin called Thor to his throne room. Thor knew that something was wrong. His father rarely summoned him in such a harsh tone. Thor was sure that his jealous brother Loki had spun some lie to get him into trouble.

But nothing could have been further from Thor's mind than what Odin had to say to him.

Odin told Thor that he was his favoured son.

He told him that he was brave beyond compare and noble as a prince must be.

He told him that his strength was legendary and that he was the best warrior in the kingdom.

But Thor did not know what it meant to be weak or to feel pain. And without knowing humility, Thor could never be a truly honourable warrior.

Odin was angry. In his rage, he tore Mjolnir from Thor's hand and threw it towards Midgard. Then he stripped Thor of his armour and sent him to Earth.

Odin made his son believe that he was a medical student with an injured leg, named Don Blake.

As Blake, Thor learned to study hard. At times he thought he might fail. But he worked harder than he ever had in Asgard and in the end he earned his degree.

He allowed others to help him with his injury. In doing so, he discovered that people were generally good. Thor learned to truly love humanity. As a surgeon, he treated the sick.

He helped weak people find their strengths.

And one day, while on holiday in Norway ...

... Don Blake found himself trapped in a cave. The only possible exit lay behind a boulder.

He found a staff on the ground and shoved it under the boulder. He tried with all his might to move the rock. He pushed and pushed.

Nothing.

He was so angry that he took the staff and struck it on the ground. And that's when it became clear that it was no ordinary stick.

It was Mjolnir in disguise!

Odin had sent Don to this cave. Odin, the All Father of Asgard, was pleased.

His son had learned humility.

He had at long last become a complete hero.

He had become human in spirit, but still, now and forever ...

he was
THE MIGHTY THOR.

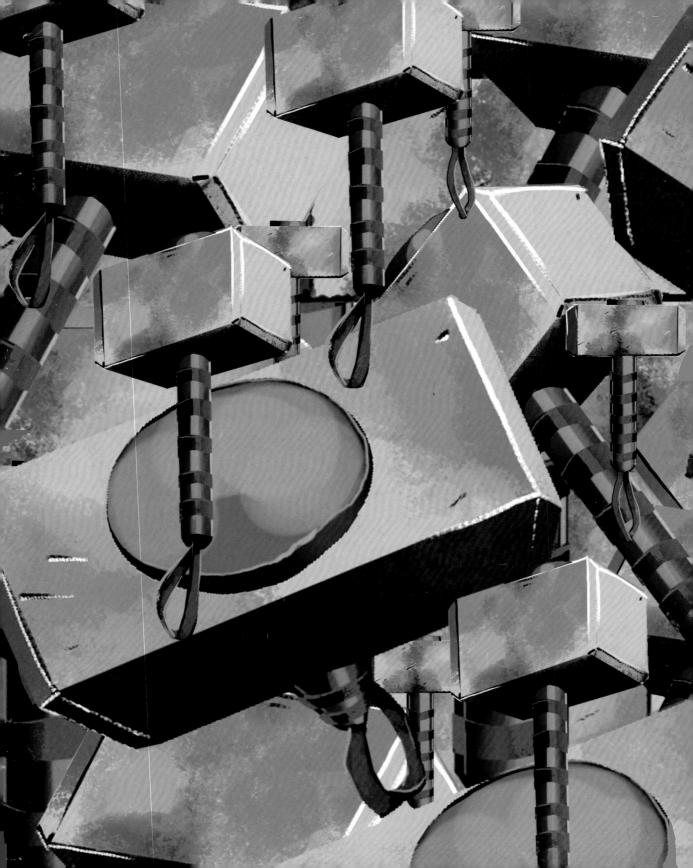